LOCKDOWN FANTASY #3

Compiled & Edited by
D. Kershaw | Maggie Pawsey | S.N. Graves

Also available and coming soon from Black Hare Press

DARK DRABBLES ANTHOLOGIES

WORLDS	APOCALYPSE
ANGELS	LOVE
MONSTERS	HATE
BEYOND	OCEANS
UNRAVEL	ANCIENTS

BHP WRITERS' GROUP SPECIAL EDITIONS

STORMING AREA 51
EERIE CHRISTMAS
BAD ROMANCE
TWENTY TWENTY

OTHER VOLUMES
DEEP SPACE
WHAT IF?
KEY TO THE KINGDOM
DEEP SEA
BEYOND THE REALM

Twitter: @BlackHarePress
Facebook: BlackHarePress
Website: www.BlackHarePress.com

LOCKDOWN FANTASY #3 title is
Copyright © 2020 Black Hare Press
First published in Australia in December 2020 by Black Hare
Press

The authors of the individual stories retain the copyright of the
works featured in this anthology

*All characters and events in this publication, other than those
clearly in the public domain, are fictitious and any resemblance
to real persons, living or dead, is purely coincidental.*

All rights reserved. No part of this production may be
reproduced, stored in a retrieval system, or transmitted, in any
form or by any means, electronic, mechanical, photocopying,
recording or otherwise, without the prior permission of the
publisher and copyright owner.

Paperback : ISBN 978-0-6450739-1-1

Cover Design	Dawn Burdett	www.dmburdett.com
Formatting	Ben Thomas	www.blackharepress.com
Editing	D. Kershaw	www.blackharepress.com
	Maggie Pawsey	
	S.N. Graves	www.sngraves.com
Read Team	Alice Lam	www.alicelambooks.com
	David Green	davidgreenwritercom.wordpress.com
	Holley Cornetto	
	Jennifer Hatfield	jhatfieldauthor.wixsite.com/website
	Jodi Jensen	jodijensenwrites.wordpress.com
	Lyndsay Ellis-Holloway	authorlyndseyellisholloway.webador.co.uk
	Stacey Jaine McIntosh	www.staceyjainemcintosh.com

TABLE OF CONTENTS

HOURS ON THE VOODOO CLOCK

By Kelly Matsuura

"What time is it, Miss Lavergne?" the big New Caledonian man asked me again. He shielded his eyes from the sun and changed his sitting position. We were riding together in the back of a small utility truck with several suitcases and a large pine coffin. There was no escape from the burning heat. Or each other.

"Stop asking me." Two days with him and now this rattling truck was too much. I couldn't wait to get back to my sister Grete's house on the north shore.

"We'll be there soon." I twisted around so I was facing the coffin, and not him directly. I leaned back against a battered suitcase and pulled my feet away from the wooden casket. I didn't want to touch it, even with sneakers on. I feared the magic.

And I didn't want Claude to wake early.

I cast an old spell on him, the kind my mother had taught me, but insisted I *never* use. If she had still been alive, she'd surely have locked me in there with Claude as punishment for misusing my power. I shuddered at the thought of being pressed against the man, another giant.

"What happens if the clock-thingy stops?" Basile asked me. I wanted to punch him.

"The clock is fine. I'll know if anything goes wrong. Relax." I had used a 1904 Jennings mantle clock, hard to find, but it had the type of mechanisms required for the spell. I replaced inner parts with snips of silver and wiring from Claude's jewellery and slowed it down to give us time to get him home. I placed some of his hair and blood inside the back of the clock as well. The most important part, the hour hand, was embedded in Claude's shoulder. It worked like a voodoo nail or arrow, but he would revive when the clock stopped, whether it was removed or not.

Basile put in earphones to listen to his iPod and closed his eyes. Finally, some peace.

I adjusted my sunhat and covered my bare legs with a sarong. I'm mixed blood, and have dark caramel skin, but I still burn after hours exposed.

I drank some water and looked at my nails. I had painted them black for Claude's funeral, but realised they wouldn't be suitable for his wedding. I would have to re-do them.

I cursed my sister again. She's not the one who had to fly to Fiji, fake a man's death, and lug him back home. But Grete gets what Grete wants. She's the only one of us four sisters that doesn't have The Gift and she makes up for it by somehow always being in charge.

And as for Claude, I never liked him much. After he disappeared, I would never have thought of him again if it wasn't for Grete constantly pining for him. She wouldn't give up hope he'd return. Seven years passed before we found out where he was and why he'd left.

I met his wife at the funeral—a pretty Indian woman a good many years younger than him. But when I squeezed her hand, I felt her pure love for Claude and knew it was returned. Theirs was not some arranged marriage like many in the Islands.

It was hard to look into her eyes, knowing I'd broken her heart. Worse, knowing Claude would spend the rest of his life married to my sister and would not remember her at all.

There was still the bonding spell to be done. I had hoped to do it first and then kill Claude, but things happened fast, and he almost overpowered me. I knew that when he woke, he'd be groggy and disoriented; he wouldn't remember who he was or what had happened in Fiji, for at least half an hour. That's when I would do it.

Or maybe I wouldn't. Maybe I'd deliver him to Grete and wash my hands of the whole thing. That's what I knew I *should* do. But I thought of my father, a good man. Not rational or just perhaps, but as loyal to his family as any person I've ever known. He would have wanted Grete to be happy, to have the man she loved, more than she wanted to live herself.

I'd never loved someone like that, but I understood the meaning of family and keeping promises. I decided I'd do the bonding spell on Claude, but wouldn't stay for the wedding. I'd go back to Fiji and make things right with Padmavati. I vowed to find her a good man, far better than Claude. And maybe one for myself too.

If I could spell one man to bond with a woman, I could spell two more.

First published in *Whispering Woods*, BWWP Publishing, 2014

THE COST OF A WISH

By Holley Cornetto

It was 1988, and my parents had been living apart for a little over a year. Because my Mom had taken on more shifts at work, I found myself spending more time at my grandma's house with my cousins. One afternoon, when my cousins and I were sitting around bored, Sam and Mike convinced me to come explore the woods behind our grandma's house. Her warning rang out from the back porch where she sat on her rocker: *"Look out for unmarked wells. You'll fall in one if you ain't careful."*

We raced our bikes down the old woods road, which was divided into three sections that ran from clearing to clearing. The first clearing was an old dumping ground for what seemed like all the cars my grandpa and uncles had ever owned. The cars sat, a graveyard of rust and oil, waiting for the day my uncles would finally work on them. Most of them ended up there in the first place because my uncles had worked on them.

The second clearing was little more

than an old stagnant pond by the right side of the road. The area was overgrown, and the pond itself only good for breeding mosquitoes and cottonmouths.

The third clearing was as far as we ever ventured. It opened into a wide field, which still held the dilapidated remains of a wooden barn. We took large sticks and searched for any sign of my grandmother's wells but weren't able to find one. The third clearing would become our base, our command-central for the games we invented.

A few days later, Sam and Mike caught me crying at grandma's house. It was Heather again. She'd spent most of elementary school making my life miserable and, now, junior high was even worse. On that particular day, she had taken one look at my clothes and led the class in a chorus of "Katey doesn't match."

Being boys, my cousins didn't understand why I cared about my clothes matching, but they wanted to make me feel better. Even though they were older, and usually balked at my childish suggestions, today they humoured me by agreeing to head to the third clearing for a game of hide-and-seek. Sam counted first. Since it was my turn to hide, I searched around the borders, looking for a place we hadn't yet explored.

In the northwest corner, obscured by an overgrowth of honeysuckle and bittersweet, there was a large arched trellis, half rotten, that formed a tunnel leading deeper into the forest. The overgrowth was so thick that I couldn't see around it, so I pulled away a few vines and crept inside. I sat for a while, waiting for Sam to wander over. When I was finally bored of waiting, and my calves ached from crouching, I turned and looked toward the far end of the tunnel.

Although the opening of the trellis was overgrown, the pathway was clear beyond it. I could see straight through to the opposite end, and what looked like another clearing. I was excited by the prospect of a new, secret place. I decided that unless Sam or Mike found me, I wouldn't tell them about my passage.

I made my way through the tunnel of rotting wood and vines. At first glimpse, the archway hadn't seemed very long. The cloying scent of honeysuckle was dizzying, making the humid air seem thicker. Farther down the tunnel, the old, rotten wood gave way to posts that were new and well kept. The plants hanging from the top were no longer unruly vines, but beautifully cultivated wisteria.

I heard a soft rustling noise, although there was no breeze. I stopped and listened, thinking Sam or Mike had uncovered my hiding place. My ears strained to make out the faint sounds. It wasn't coming from the entrance to the trellis, but from all around me. And it wasn't rustling; it was murmuring.

"Who is there?" My voice came out as barely a whisper.

Whoisthere? Whoisthere? Whoisthere?

repeated a soft echo.

"Mike?" I tried a little louder. "Sam?"

Whoisthere? Whoisthere? Whoisthere?

I stepped out to find myself in what looked like someone's garden. There was a stone bench beside the trellis, and a path of paving stones led to a well in the centre. The garden, for that is what it must have been, was weeded and maintained to perfection. Small trees with pink and white flowers stood in a circle around the well. A part of me couldn't help but recall my grandmother's warning about abandoned wells. I looked for a path that might lead me to the home of the garden's owner, but there was only the one that led me here.

A light fog covered the ground just enough to obscure my feet. I walked around, glancing at the lilies and coneflowers that bordered the garden. Although there were no walls, the place felt completely enclosed. The stargazer lilies emanated a strong, sweet smell. The colours were more vivid than any flower I'd ever seen.

"It's about time," came a voice from behind me.

I turned to see a woman sitting on the bench. I was certain she hadn't been there before, and yet I wasn't surprised to see her there. As a matter of fact, I wasn't surprised to enter the garden. The flowers, the smells, they all seemed strangely familiar to me.

"Is this your garden? I'm sorry. I didn't know this was here. It's beautiful."

The woman grunted in reply.

I approached the bench, hoping that if I

drew close enough, I might recognise her. She looked ancient. Her body was small and gnarled. At eleven years old, I was sure that I was taller than her. I gasped as I looked at her face. She had no visible pupils, no irises. Nothing but pure white orbs.

She must have heard my gasp, because she laughed. "They say that eyes are the window to the soul. If it's true, what does that mean for me?"

"I…I don't know." I started backing up.

"Don't run from me, child. I've been waiting for you to come."

I nodded. Of course she was waiting for me. That strange feeling of familiarity washed over me again.

"This is your garden now. Take better care than I did."

"But, you do take good care of it. The plants are lovely."

"It isn't the plants that you need to worry about." She pointed a gnarled finger at the wishing well.

I approached the well and glanced inside, unable to see the bottom through the darkness. Vines with berries as red as tomatoes snaked up the stones around it. It was the only sign of neglect in the garden. I glanced back at the woman. "What does a wish cost?"

"More than you can imagine."

I turned back, undaunted by her words. "All things come with a cost."

"Perhaps it costs a strand of hair. Perhaps a fingernail clipping. Perhaps it costs something you've already lost."

"That doesn't make any sense."

"Or perhaps it costs a precious memory. Perhaps your right hand. Perhaps it costs something that you'll never have."

I started to worry for the woman, sure she was talking nonsense. "How long have you been out here? Can I get someone for you?"

She shook her head. "You are the one I waited for."

It seemed impossible. The garden, the woman, the well. When I turned back to the bench, she was gone.

Unobserved by human eyes, I gazed into the well again. "If only…"

Ifonly. Ifonly. Ifonly. The sound emanated from the fathoms below.

"I suppose it can't hurt to try."

Hurttotry. Hurttotry. Hurttotry.

"Oh, shut up!" I shook my finger toward the darkness. "You could at least say something useful."

I gazed back down at the well. What I wanted more than anything was for my parents to get back together. I hated how empty my house felt, and how many hours Mom spent at her job. I closed my eyes, and I wished.

When I emerged from the garden, the sun was setting. "Sam? Mike?"

"Katey!" I saw them charge down the path toward me. "We looked everywhere. Didn't you hear us yell? We were heading home. Thought you snuck off as a joke."

I shook my head and pointed to the trellis. "I was over there. I didn't hear you calling me."

They both looked as if they didn't believe me, but I *hadn't* heard them calling. I didn't know how to explain where I'd been.

"Whatever, Katey. We didn't want to play hide and seek anyway. Next time, we pick the game."

I nodded, and the three of us set out for home.

The next day when I got home from school, my mom was nowhere to be found. I thought it odd that she wasn't home, since it was her day off, but continued to the kitchen where I grabbed a banana off the counter and noticed a note taped to the fridge.

Katey,

I'm having dinner with your father tonight. You can go to Grandma's if you need anything. Money in the canister.

Love,

Mom

When I got to Grandma's, my cousins were waiting for me. We grabbed our bikes and headed back to our clearing. The whole time that we rode, my heart raced. I was bursting to tell them about the trellis, and the garden beyond it. I decided to show them. I wanted to see the look on their faces when they saw it.

"Guys, I want to show you something."

"Yeah?" asked Sam.

"Remember yesterday, when we were out here playing, and you couldn't find me?"

Mike rolled his eyes. "Rub it in, why don't you?"

"No, seriously. This is important. I found something."

"What did you find?"

"It's over here." I said, leading them to the corner of the clearing where the trellis stood.

The trellis stood exactly as I remembered it. Honeysuckle mixed with bittersweet snaked up the sides, seeming to hold the structure in place. It was as if the vines had grown back in overnight. They had filled back in so completely that once again I couldn't see the path beyond leading to the garden. Sam and Mike helped me pull the weeds away.

"Oh, cool!" Sam grinned.

"Yeah, just wait until you see what's inside." I stepped under the trellis. Mike and Sam followed, but there was no tunnel, no pathway. It was a simple half-rotten arch, held up by vines and weeds.

"Is that poison oak?" Mike asked.

"No, this isn't right. It's supposed to…" I pushed back some of the vines, but there was nothing.

"Supposed to what?" Sam asked.

"It leads further in. Or, at least it did yesterday."

Mike blew a raspberry. "Is this another one of your little kid games? Seriously, Katey. You need to grow up."

"I swear to God, I went in there yesterday and wished for Mom and Dad to get back together, and today they're going out to dinner."

"Quit yanking our chain. The arch is cool. We could make a game with it without all the stupid make-believe crap."

"It isn't crap, Mike!"

"Katey, nothing's there. Say what you want, but I don't see anything besides poison oak that I ain't gonna touch."

"I'm not…"

Mike held up his hand. "It ain't funny. Come on, Sam, we're going home"

"Mike!" I slumped to the ground as they headed back down the woods road without me.

I'd never fought with my cousins before. We argued from time to time, but they'd never turned their backs on me. I started after them, needing to explain, but stopped in my tracks. I had a better idea. I would show them.

I walked back to the trellis and tore down the vines. The arched pathway appeared in front of me just as before. I marched forward, coming out, once again, in the garden. The bench was still there, the plants, the wishing well. The only thing missing was the old woman.

I approached the well.

"I need help."

Help. Help. Help.

I shivered at the familiar echo.

Sam's birthday was next week, and I knew he'd been asking for a new bike. "I need to prove that you're real. I wish that Sam would get the bike he wants for his birthday."

Youarereal. Youarereal.

***

The week passed slowly. My mom spent most of her free time going out with my dad. When I asked, she'd say they were "working things out." My cousins were quiet and didn't want to play with me. Anytime I suggested we ride out, they made excuses or told me they didn't have time to play little kid games.

I approached Sam the day before his birthday. "I know you don't believe me, but I wished on the well that you'd get the bike for your birthday. If you get it, that means that the wish came true, and you'll have to believe me about the well."

"Jesus, Katey, not that again. Would you stop it? If you want to tell stories, go get your notebook and write them down. I don't want to hear it."

I huffed and walked away, muttering. He would see. He would get that bike for his birthday, and then he'd thank me.

The next day, I went straight to my grandma's after school. Sam was riding up and down the driveway on a new mountain bike, Mike trailing behind him, begging for a turn to try it.

I smirked and rode down the hill, stopping in front of the house. "Told you so."

Sam pulled in behind me and slid to a stop, testing the brakes. "Told me so, what?"

"That you would get the bike."

He rolled his eyes. "No shit, Sherlock. I asked for it."

Grandma raised her head from her crocheting. "Language, young man."

"Yes ma'am. Sorry."

I lowered my voice. "Yeah, you asked for it. But, your dad said he couldn't afford it. You got it because I wished for it."

"Bullshit."

"SAM."

"Sorry, Grandma."

"Where is your dad, anyway?"

"He's on the road 'til tonight. Grandma said he left it here for me last week. She put it up until today."

"See? That proves it."

"How does that prove anything?"

"He got it for you when I made my wish. Last week."

Sam shook his head. "You really don't

know when to quit. I don't believe you, and I'm not going to believe you, so shut up about it or go home."

I climbed back on my bike. "Happy birthday, Sam," I mumbled as I rode away.

I didn't see Sam or Mike at all that weekend. I decided it was best to stay away from my grandma's house in case they were there. I couldn't bear the way Sam looked at me anymore.

With my mom busy and my cousins avoiding me, I was lonely. I considered visiting the well and wishing things right again, but it seemed that no good had come from wishing so far, even if they *had* come true. I'd have to be careful how I made my wishes going forward.

At school, I sat at my desk thinking. I

doodled a picture of the well and, beneath it, I wrote potential wishes. I checked and revised each one, adding notes in parentheses. *I wish my Mom and Dad were back together* (and had time for me). *I wish Sam and Mike would believe me* (about the wishing well). These were things I could wish for, and if I worded the wishes just right, then I could fix things.

Without warning, the paper was jerked off my desk.

"What's this?"

I looked up to see Heather studying my scribblings. "Nothing."

"Oh, so I can throw it away?" She crumpled the paper into a ball.

"No, stop that!" I tried to grab the paper, but she waved it teasingly beyond my reach.

"So it *isn't* nothing, then?"

"It's nothing to you."

She unwadded the paper and looked at it. "What kind of stupid shit is this? A wishing well? What are you, five years old?"

"None of your business," I said, reaching for the paper. "Give it back." I could feel my eyes tearing up.

She held it out so she could see it. "Boohoo, I want my mommy and daddy to love me. Even my family hates me. Poor me. I wish I had friends."

"It works," I said, and then covered my mouth with my hand. *Stupid.*

She burst out laughing. "Yeah, and I'll bet you still believe in Santa Claus, too. I knew you were weird, but I didn't think you were a baby."

"I'm not."

She laughed harder. "Don't worry, I'll take care of this for you."

By that afternoon, the whole class knew. She'd invented a new rhyme for them to sing, "Crazy Katey, such a baby. Lives alone up on a hill, has no friends and never will."

I got off the bus that afternoon in tears. I headed straight back to the clearing, straight back to the trellis hiding in the bittersweet vine.

There was only one thing that I wanted.

The vines murmured as I ran through the arched path. I grabbed the sides of the well and doubled over to catch my breath.

"Have you used its power enough to recognise its cost?"

The woman sat on the bench behind me, looking as she had the first time I'd seen her.

"Is that what happened to your eyes?" I asked.

She nodded.

"How long have you been here?"

"Oh, a few seconds, or a few days. Maybe even years. But certainly a lifetime."

"You always say things in riddles."

She nodded. "Such is my curse. I must answer your questions, and yet I cannot."

"Are you here to tell me something?"

"I am here so that you will see, as I could not. The last wish pays for all."

"But I've already paid. I wanted my

parents to get back together, and now I never see them. I wished for my cousin to get the bike he wanted, but now he hates me. I've lost everyone I care about. What else can I lose?"

She stared at the well with her milky eyes. "It isn't too late until it's too late."

"Yeah, I get it. This is the last time I can use it. Will I lose my sight, like you?"

"Does it matter, if you're already blind?"

"Why can't you just tell me what to say? I need this wish, do you understand? I hate Heather. I hate her! I can't go one more day with her bullying me. I just wish she was gone!"

Shewasgone. Shewasgone. Shewasgone.

"Shit." I spun and looked at the well. "I

didn't mean to. It wasn't a wish." I turned back, and the bench was empty. I looked around the garden and shouted, "HOW DO I STOP IT?"

Stopit. Stopit. Stopit.

I collapsed against the cold stones of the well. I didn't know why, but I began to weep.

The next week, Heather wasn't at school. Without the constant strain of her abuse, I paid more attention in class and answered more questions. I looked my classmates in the eyes for a change. It was wonderful to finally feel free, to feel that I could be myself without fear of humiliation. But my happiness was tainted by guilt. I felt guilty because I was happy. I didn't know what happened to her, and I didn't want to find out. I wanted to remain ignorant, uncaring. If I never learned what happened, there was nothing to feel bad about, or so I told myself.

When I went to my grandmother's house one afternoon, the police were there. I saw the black bag on a stretcher being loaded into an ambulance. I'd seen enough movies to know what was inside.

My grandmother was on the porch in her rocker. For the first time I could remember, she looked old and pale. "Who…who was it, Grandma?" My heart beat so hard I was sure she could hear it. I was afraid that Sam or Mike would be in that bag.

"A girl from your school."

I must have looked relieved, because

she gave me a strange look. "She was found in one of them wells I've warned ya'll about."

"Oh. But…why was she here?"

My grandmother cocked her head, studying me. "She wasn't here to see you?"

I shook my head. "I didn't invite anybody over."

By then the officer in charge came over. He was tall and clean shaven with a crew cut. He looked exactly as I thought a policeman should.

"Your name, young lady?"

"Katey Owens."

"Do you know anything about a girl being out in the woods around here?"

I swallowed hard. His tone was pleasant, but he made me nervous. "No, sir.

Just me and my cousins. We come out here to play just about every day."

He nodded. "Did you ever have friends over?

I shook my head. "Not in a long time." I stole a glance at my grandma. When had she become so frail?

"Did either of your cousins ever talk about bringing a girl over? Bringing her into the woods?"

"No. I mean, they talked about girls…but not…like, *a* girl." My face flushed. I looked down at his shoes, which were covered in dust from Grandma's driveway. He would be taking a part of Grandma's house with him when he left. He'd deposit her dust to the other places he went.

He grunted in reply.

Somehow, I knew the girl in the body bag was Heather. Part of me felt guilt for what I had done to her, but the other part felt relieved it wasn't Sam or Mike.

My grandmother looked up from her rocker at the officer. Her arthritic hands trembled as she asked, "Are you gonna take her in, too?"

"What do you mean, too?" I asked.

"We've taken your cousins down to the station to answer some questions."

"You think they did this?" I glanced from the officer to my grandmother, who was now clutching her chest.

The cop shrugged. "It's too soon to think much of anything."

Grandma gasped for air, tremors

wracking her body.

The officer called for a medic.

"Shit. Shit. Shit."

Tunnel vision closed in, and everything around me was painted in darkness.

By the time I came around, they were loading my grandmother into an ambulance. There was a paramedic sitting beside me.

"Slow, deep breaths. That-a-girl. You fainted." The paramedic smiled down at me, but it wasn't reassuring.

Seeing me awake, the officer walked back over. "Your grandmother had a heart attack. They're taking her to the hospital. Is there somewhere we can take you, or drop you off?"

I shook my head. "I live down the street. I can ride my bike home."

He looked sceptical, but didn't argue.

I went home to an empty house and cried myself to sleep.

I spent the next few days at home. I didn't feel like going to school. My mom came by briefly, but told me that she needed to stay at the hospital with grandma. I didn't hear from Sam or Mike. I had no idea if they were being held by the police, or if they had been allowed to leave.

My grief and guilt consumed me. A prisoner of my own mind, I no longer seemed to inhabit the physical world. I laid around for days feeling sorry for myself, wallowing in my guilt.

After a week, I'd had enough. All of what happened—Heather, Sam, my grandmother—all of it had been my fault.

No one was going to fix it for me. I had to go back.

I showered, dressed, and got on my bike. My hands on the handlebars looked old and gnarled.

The clearing had been trampled by rescuers and police, leaving it naked and exposed. Part of me feared that the trellis would be gone, and that I'd never find my way back to the garden with the well.

It was still there, but knocked over, discarded in a heap of vines and debris. I lifted it carefully, afraid that the slightest movement might cause it to fall apart. I wasn't sure how, but I knew that if the trellis broke, I'd never make it back. I dragged it over to where it once stood and propped it up as best I could. It didn't look stable without the vines to brace it, but it would have to do.

I took a deep breath and stepped inside. The rotted wood was more obvious. I was sure that at any moment the trellis would fall and trap me underneath. "Hello?"

There was no echo this time.

I reached the end and stepped through. The garden was changed. The well was a half-covered hole in the ground. The only thing familiar was the creeping vines with tomato-red berries. Bits of police tape were wrapped around the ring of trees surrounding it. The beautiful array of perennials was now gone, and in their place grew dandelions and pokeweed.

"I need to make another wish. Please!"

I glanced at the bench, now a shattered

slab of rock. She wasn't there. I sat down and wept.

I couldn't say how long I sat there. I never moved from the bench. I just sat and thought about the things I'd done. I wondered if anyone would bother to look for me, if anyone missed me.

***

Time seemed frozen. Days passed. Weeks. Months. But it had been only seconds, minutes. I was finally shaken from my reverie when I heard a quiet murmur.

Whoisthere? Whoisthere?

A silhouette stepped out from the trellis and approached the well. I listened from the bench. The girl looked as I had when I first discovered the well.

"It's about time," I said to the girl.

She jumped and spun to face me.

"Is this your garden? I'm sorry. I didn't know this was here. It's beautiful."

"I've been waiting for you," I replied.

First published in *online*, Collective Realms Magazine, 2019

MIRROR MIRROR

By Stacey Jaine McIntosh

The sound of breaking glass stopped her. The mirror was broken. The shards shone like diamonds on the black tile floor. The empty ebony wood frame stood out against the pale stone wall of the queen's castle.

"Snow White!" the queen cursed, her rage growing with every passing moment. "You will pay for this with your life."

Of course, Snow wasn't responsible for breaking the mirror. If the hunter was true to his word, her heart was already in his hands. Its essence expelled.

The queen smiled.

Who is the fairest one of all?

You are, my queen. You are.

THE FIRST MAN

By Zoey Xolton

God looked down upon the Earth and all that he had created and was pleased. The land flourished, bountiful and beautiful. The forests were heavy with their burdens of fruit and blossom. Animals of every kind, both great and small, multiplied and bore young.

His vision was almost complete.

Reaching down from the heavens, he scooped up a measure of earth in his hands, and from it, he crafted his most prized of creations—Adam, the First Man. Setting his child into the garden he had created, he said, "From dust you were born, and to dust you shall return."

SYLVAN INFANTRY

By Matthew M. Montelione

Holbrook, New York.
1 August 1963.

It was a hot summer evening when eighteen-year-old Nicholas Strong heard knocking at his front door. He was too lazy to get up from the couch. He held his half-eaten sandwich in one hand and a soda in the other. "Everyday" by Buddy Holly played on the record player next to him. He was finally done working for the day, and nobody was going to intrude on his relaxation.

Knock knock knock.

"Answer the door, Sandy!" Nicholas yelled to his little sister.

Knock knock knock.

Sandy Strong came running down the stairs and rolled her eyes at Nicholas. "Would it kill you to get up? I was grooming Valens."

"Just get the door," Nicholas said with a mouthful of turkey and cheese. "The cat can wait!" Nicholas peered over as his sister opened the door.

A tall slender man with deep green eyes and a sharp nose stood there. He was roughly six feet six inches, with long brown hair that was tied back in a ponytail. He was dressed in a black suit with a cream-coloured dress shirt.

"Um…can we help you?" Sandy asked.

"I hope that you can, little one," the man said with a kind smile. His voice was deep and unusual. "My name is Everett Harding. I wish to speak with your father. Is he at home?"

Nicholas was taken aback by the man's commanding presence, but puffed out his chest and walked over to the door. He ushered Sandy behind him. "My pop's sleeping. He's a sick man and needs his rest. He doesn't take well to people who derail his slumber. What do you want?"

"I apologise if my coming offends you. I ask only for a moment of your time. I seek to offer you a deal."

Nicholas laughed. "A dishevelled salesman offering me a deal? Seems a little shady. Sorry, I'm not much into giggle-smokes."

Everett looked slightly confused. "You speak of drugs? Dear boy, I wish to buy your house and property for more than its value."

Nicholas's face turned red with rage. Their father had no plans to sell their home, where they grew up and their mother died. His breathing grew heavier. Sandy grabbed his hand. Usually, her touch helped Nicholas calm down. His breathing slowed down, and he composed himself.

"Listen, you lunatic," Nicholas said, holding back his anger, "I don't know who you are, or where you're from, but we aren't going anywhere. For the sake of my little sister, I'm not going to punch you. Now get off our property before I call the police!"

Everett's cool eyes focused on Nicholas. "As I told your more level-headed counterpart, my name is Everett Harding. I come with my request as a concerned neighbour. You see, I live beyond Hollow Brook Forest, at its north end."

"Hollow Brook Forest? What are you

talking about?" Nicholas asked.

"The woodland to your north. It was once called Hollow Brook Forest. Did you not know?"

"Here we just call it the woods. What is your concern, neighbour?" Nicholas asked sarcastically.

"Your family are loggers," Everett calmly said.

"Strong & Son Logging at your service, if you were a more decent fellow and hadn't disrupted my dinner. How does our business concern you?"

"I wish to expand my own property, as I have run into quite a lot of money. I can pay you most handsomely, thrice as much as your house and land is worth, if your father desires to sell."

Nicholas was finished with the intruding man. He grew red again, inching closer to Everett. "Get off our property, you no-good creep, before I remove you. This is your last warning. Our property is not for sale, and besides, I'm confident that you've got no such money!"

Everett backed away and bowed. "I can see that, at this moment, no deal can be made. Please forgive my intrusion." He turned and left them, travelling towards the forest.

"What a strange guy," Nicholas said.

"Yeah," Sandy said. "Did he walk here through the woods?"

"Who cares? Good riddance," Nicholas answered, shutting the door.

"Why would he want to buy our

house?"

"I don't know. Just forget him, Sandy. Listen, go upstairs and check on Dad. He needs his medication soon."

"Dad is doing just fine, and can get his own medicine," Louis Strong said, slowly making his way down the stairs.

"Dad!" Sandy exclaimed, running over to her aged father. "Let me help you."

"Thank you, sweetheart. Who was at the door, Nicholas?"

"Some idiot who said he lived north of the woods. He asked to buy our house! Can you believe it?! He offered me three times what it's worth, but he was full of it. Nobody has that kind of cash to throw around! I should have popped him right in the nose," Nicholas said regretfully.

Louis smiled, placing his hand on Nicholas's shoulder. "Calm down, son. We don't know this man or what he's worth. Maybe he works in the oil industry. Either way, you did right in rejecting his offer. Your mother loved this house. I'll be damned if I see it sold."

Nicholas lightened up and smiled. "Alright, Dad," he said.

"Come on," Louis said, "our program is on soon. We can't miss a second of it!"

"I'll make the coffee!" Sandy said, dashing off.

The next morning, Nicholas awoke to the smell of omelettes. Over breakfast, he and his family talked about their mother who died of cancer. Nicholas remembered her, but Sandy was only two years old when it happened. It upset him to talk about her, but when he did, he felt like it introduced her to Sandy, and brought her closer to them, although she was gone. Nicholas started getting teary-eyed.

"Well, I have to go," he said, fighting his emotions. "I'm in the field today, and those guys need as much help as they can get. Sandy, go feed Valens. He always enjoys an early breakfast," Nicholas said, kissing his little sister on her head.

"Come back soon!" Sandy yelled as she went off to feed the cat.

Louis looked downtrodden.

"What's wrong?" Nicholas asked.

"You know that I'd be out there with you if I wasn't sick."

Nicholas put his hand on his father's

shoulder. "I know, Dad. But you don't need to worry about a thing. You started this company with your bare hands, and you know that I'll take care of it for you. Always. At least until you're back to your old self again." Louis smiled.

Before he shut the door, Nicholas heard Sandy run to the top of the stairs. "Have you guys seen Valens? He's not in his bed."

"He's a cat," Louis said. "He could be in any nook of the house. Come on," he said, "whoever finds him first is off of clean-up duty!"

Nicholas smiled, shutting the door behind him.

Later, Nicholas wiped the sweat from his brow as the scorching afternoon sun beat down on him and his team. "Ugh," he said to his close friend Randy Hughes, "it's way too hot out. This humidity sucks."

"It'll be like this all summer, Nick. If you're on Long Island in August, you might as well prepare yourself to be drenched in your own sweat every day," Randy said, exhausted. "At least it's almost time to go home."

For hours, Nicholas had toiled in the fields, felling trees and hauling wood from the bordering forest. He was dirty, hungry, and ready to leave. Finally, five o'clock came and Nicholas picked up his chainsaw near the border of the woods. As he turned to head to his truck, he caught a quick glimpse of orange in a sea of green. He turned to the woods, looking closer.

Staring. He suddenly turned deathly pale; his jaw dropped in horror. Valens, the family cat, hung from a noose tied around the limb of a thick oak tree.

"No! No!" Nicholas yelled, running over to his lifeless pet and removing the rope from around his neck. He cradled him as he took him to his truck and placed him on the passenger seat. Overcome by grief, he curled up on the ground, weeping uncontrollably for the first time since his mother passed away. The family loved Valens. What was he going to tell his little sister? Who would do such a thing to a family's cat? Sandy was only fourteen years old and innocent to unexpected horrors. Should he tell her the truth about how he found Valens?

Nicholas's coworkers soon came to his side, joining him in his grief when they realised what had happened.

"What kind of lowlife would do this?" Randy asked angrily.

"Don't worry, Nick. We'll find out who did it," another coworker said. "They'll pay. Is anybody after you?"

"I didn't think so," Nicholas muttered through his tears. He stood up, wiping his face. "But whoever it was just made an enemy beyond his wildest dreams. And you're damn right. Whoever it was is going to pay."

Two weeks passed by until the family started rebounding from their beloved pet's death. Nicholas had lied to Sandy and told her that Valens was hit by a car. He couldn't bring himself to tell her the hard truth. She was inconsolable for many days, but lately started to come out of her shell. Nicholas told Louis the truth, of course, but he wished that he had not. Louis became increasingly anxious and worried about his family's safety. Nicholas did not admit it to Sandy, but deep down, he was worried too. After all, Valens's information was on his tag—he was clearly a house cat who belonged to them. Nicholas racked his brain, trying to think of who would commit such a heinous act. He made enemies in the past, but he had assumed those scores were scttled. Besides, murder of a family pet was beyond any reasonable form of revenge. This was a clear, point-blank blow. A declaration of war.

One night, while the family was eating dinner, Nicholas grew anxious, thinking about the unknown villain who killed Valens.

"I miss Valens," Sandy said. "Remember how he jumped onto my lap when I ate? He would always try to get some of my meal."

"And he'd get it too," Louis chuckled.

A knocking at the door broke the sad silence that followed the brief laughter.

Knock knock knock.

"Who's disrupting our dinner?" Nicholas asked, getting up. "I hate when people interrupt dinner."

"Take it easy, Nicholas. Not everyone eats dinner when we do, you know," Louis said.

Knock knock knock.

Nicholas walked over to the door and opened it. His temper flared when he saw Everett Harding standing before him, dressed in the same suit he was in weeks ago. "You again! I thought I told you we aren't interested in selling?"

"Hello, sir. Can I have another moment of your time?" Everett asked politely.

"Well, as you can see, we're in the middle of dinner. But since I'm at the door and you are already wasting my time, what is it that you want now? My first-born child?"

Louis slowly got up and walked towards the door.

"I would like to once again extend my

offer to buy your property for an exuberant sum of money. This time, I offer you six times what it is worth. Do you desire more?" Everett asked.

Nicholas was furious. "I already told you! We aren't selling our house! Who even asks that when there's no sale sign? If you're not out of here in five seconds, I'm getting my baseball bat. Then you'll be sorry you came again!"

Everett calmly stood his ground.

Louis put his arm around Nicholas. "Go cool off, son. I'll handle this."

"But Dad, this guy's as thick as a brick. I told him we aren't selling."

"Just go. I'll take it from here." Louis flashed Nicholas a stern look, the type Nicholas had not seen since he was a little boy.

"Fine," Nicholas relented, walking back to the table, staring Everett down on the way.

"Don't worry about it, Nick," Sandy said. "Dad will take care of it."

Louis stood up tall. "Why have you come, mister...?"

"Mr Everett Harding, my fine sir. How do you do?"

"My children told me that you are a neighbour?"

"Indeed. I live on the northern borders of the forest. It is a beautiful area, but I fear it has become too small for me. You see, I am in the middle of a grand enterprise to expand my borders. I seek to own all of Hollow Brook Forest. Your property stands in the way of my venture, and so I wish to purchase it at a price six times what it is worth."

Louis stared at the towering man before him, remaining silent for a few moments, seemingly contemplating the deal.

"I am sorry to hear about your cat," Everett added.

Nicholas came to his father's side in a rage. "How do you know about Valens?!"

"Holbrook is a small town. News travels fast, especially between neighbours. Usually, after a tragedy, families look to move on from the place in which the said tragedy occurred. Is it possible that there is such a case here?"

"You insensitive son of a bitch,"

Nicholas said. He was ready to strike Everett, but his father put his arm in front of him.

"Thanks for your concern, neighbour. I won't lie, your offer is enticing. How do I know you're good for such a sum?" Louis replied calmly.

Nicholas was furious. "Are you really thinking about selling our house to this madman?" he asked his father.

Everett reached into his pockets and pulled out wads of hundred-dollar bills. "I am very wealthy, Mr Strong. And I can pay it all in cash." There had to be thousands of dollars on his person alone. Nicholas was silently impressed.

"Pray tell, Mr Harding," Louis started, "for I am a sentimental man. What would you do with our home, if we were to sell? We've made many memories here, and as you can see, we're loggers who own a booming business on our doorstep, one that we cannot easily find elsewhere. The timber here provides us with much revenue."

Everett's green eyes suddenly flared under his thick eyebrows and his kindly face sharpened into a scowl. "Provides you with revenue? Ha! I'll tell you what I would do. I would irrevocably shut down your miserable operation and immediately see to it that seeds are planted where once there were tall trees—living beings that you so foolishly ripped away from the Earth!" Everett stood tall and proud; his voice bellowed through the house. "Day by day, you encroach upon the northern reaches of Hollow Brook Forest with your axes, chainsaws, and other mechanisms of folly! I will have it no longer! You must go! Take the money and go!"

"You'll pay for that!" Nicholas yelled, cocking his arm back, and punching Everett in his face. Everett leaned over with a bloody nose.

Louis was flustered. "How dare you, coming to my home, insulting me and my family! Next time I see you on my property, I'll call the police! Do you understand me?!" he yelled, slamming the door in Everett's face.

"Can you believe that jerk, trying to use our cat's death as an excuse for us to sell?" Nicholas asked. "If he comes here again, I'm bashing his brains in with my bat."

"And go to jail for murder, so that when I die your little sister will be left without a provider?" Louis asked his son. Nicholas hung his head in shame.

Sandy threw her arms around her father. "I hate that man! Don't let him come here again, Daddy. He gives me the creeps!"

"We won't give him the time of day ever again, sweetheart," Louis said. "If he sets foot on this property, you call the cops. Do you hear me? We can't take our chances with somebody like that, kind one moment and crazy the next."

Later that night, the family went about their usual activities, but Nicholas couldn't shake the altercation with Everett Harding from his mind.

A couple of weeks later, Louis died of his illness. The Strong children blamed Everett for pushing their father's stress levels over the edge. Nicholas went through hell, planning the wake and funeral and sorting through his belongings. Inconsolable depression ruled his life. Months blurred together; Nicholas walked about in a daze with little care for the happenings of the outside world. He continued in this fashion until August 1964, when the weather felt even hotter than the year prior, and Louis's younger sister Dorothy decided to fly up from Florida and stay with her nephew and niece for an undetermined amount of time.

Nicholas was not too happy about that, for now at nineteen years old he was the legal head-of-the-household charged with taking care of Sandy and managing the entire estate and business. He was determined to handle his new responsibilities without any interference from family members, especially from his aunt who would undoubtedly act like a babysitter. However, Nicholas's actions did not prove to anyone that he was ready for the task at hand.

Since his father's death, he drank alcohol in excess and continually spiralled into intoxicated rages that grew worse by the day. He smashed random objects against the wall in his room and often went outside to beat his baseball bat against trees in the yard. Sandy's efforts failed to comfort him.

One night, while Aunt Dorothy stayed with a friend, Nicholas lay on his bed in a drunken haze. He heard the loud television—Sandy was watching some silly program. He gazed out the window at the rising full moon. He thought he heard his sister call out to him, but he ignored her, drifting into an uneasy sleep.

Nicholas awoke to his sister's cries. He gripped his empty whiskey bottle close to his chest. Once he processed what was going on, he sprang up from his bed.

"Sandy?" he yelled, recalling the hazy calls of his sister before he passed out.

No answer.

He ran downstairs and saw the

television set left on; the door was wide open. His heart raced. He quickly grabbed a kitchen knife, dashing out of his house and into the road. For a moment he did not move, unsure of which way to go. At that very moment, he heard Sandy scream again. It sounded like her screams were coming from the lumberyard, near the forest.

Nicholas raced north through the field of fallen trees, dodging and jumping over stumps, pits, and machinery. Sandy screamed ahead.

"I'll save you Sandy! I'll save you!" he yelled, running towards the sounds of her cries. The hot and clammy night air soaked his skin. He panted.

He reached the thickly wooded

boundary of his family's land. All was dark within the forest. Sandy screamed again. He was much closer to her now. She had to be in the woods.

"I'm coming, Sandy!" Nicholas yelled. Just as he stepped into the wood, a tall and cryptic figure emerged from the blackness in front of him. Nicholas stood fast, tightening his grasp on his knife. He held it close, waiting for the right moment to strike.

"You will listen, boy, if you care about your sister's safety," a familiar voice said. Nicholas realised that Everett Harding stood before him. He now understood the horror of the entire situation. It had to be Everett who killed Valens, who expedited his father's death, and now abducted his little sister.

"I'll rip you apart!" Nicholas screamed, lunging towards Everett.

With abnormal quickness, Everett dodged Nicholas's attack and punched him in the stomach. The blow hit harder than any school yard punch Nicholas had ever experienced. He fell to the ground, writhing in pain.

"I gave you many chances to accept my proposal. I even gave you an excuse to leave! Yet, you did not listen!" Everett kicked Nicholas and circled around him like an eagle to its prey. He towered over the young man. His eyes, which were once normal in size, now blazed a brilliant emerald colour and grew in diameter. "At least…you did not listen to me in human form."

Nicholas lifted his woozy head, peering at the strange sight before him. He thought he saw what looked like a veil of water stream over Everett for a few seconds. What appeared in the man's place following this brief transition chilled Nicholas to his core.

"Will this one do the trick?!" A deeper voice not entirely unlike Everett's bellowed.

In Everett's place was no man. He resembled a man in some ways, but he was not human. He was broader than Everett and had brown skin that shone like silk in the moonlight. Two slender curved horns about twelve inches high protruded from his forehead. Dark brown hair fell about his shoulders.

"Now you see me, human. I am Deacon, an ancient spirit of Hollow Brook Forest. Your disgusting family, along with many others of your kind, have provoked us for far too long. You destroy our homes, and your grotesque greed appals us!" Deacon proudly looked skyward. The bright moon reflected in his large eyes. "Each and every summer, when our powers are greatest, we of the Sylvan infantry discuss what to do about the human plague. But the time for talk is over. This summer, we are mobilising. There is a war coming, Nicholas Strong. A war for dominion of this good planet, a planet that your fledgling race readily destroys. I admit, I was sceptical about whether or not humans could be reasoned with, but you answered that question for me last summer. Your race is far too stubborn to co-exist with us."

The creature pointed to the dark forest. "Hollow Brook Forest is ours! Your sister is my prisoner. I will raise her as one of the Sylvan people. She will be cared for. But rest assured, when you see her next, if you ever do, she will not be on your side."

Nicholas watched in shock and agony as Deacon turned from him and walked towards the woods, towards his screaming sister. He could not abandon her! He would rather die than let Sandy fall victim to this murderer! "No…wait! Wait!" he shouted, "take me instead! Take me!"

Deacon stopped, cocking his head. "Now you want to strike a deal, hm?"

"Take me instead!" Nicholas yelled as he slowly rose. "I am strong and can work for long hours. I am a fighter!"

Deacon turned towards Nicholas. "Your rage may be your only admirable trait. Properly channelled, you could be an able warrior." The beast was silent for a moment, as if in thought. "Do you swear fealty to the Sylvan race? Your word is bound under pain of death."

Nicholas sighed. "If it means my sister goes free, unharmed, and is allowed to continue her life without your interference…then yes, I swear it with my whole heart."

"Ha," Deacon smiled. "Good. She was here the whole time, you know," Deacon said, pointing to his left. "She is unharmed."

Suddenly, a watery veil lifted, and Sandy appeared. True to his word, she was not hurt.

"Nicholas!" she yelled, weeping as she ran towards him. "He took me from our house!"

"Sandy!" he said, tightly hugging her. "I'm so sorry that I wasn't there to protect you. I know this doesn't make sense, but you have to trust me. I have to go."

"What? No!" Sandy argued.

Deacon grew impatient. "The deal is done! Come now, Nicholas. Your training begins immediately."

The young man obeyed and turned to Sandy. "Goodbye, little sister. Remember, I love you. I'm doing this because I love you."

Deacon bent down towards Sandy and smiled. "Fear not, child. Your brother will make a fine soldier in our ranks and will wage war upon your kind soon enough."

Nicholas heard Sandy's cries as he followed the creature into the dark abyss of Hollow Brook Forest.

First published in *Summer's Splash*, Fantasia Divinity, 2019

HOSTEL TAKEOVER

By John H. Dromey

When a travel-weary couple arrived late at night in a picturesque English coastal village, the only lodging available to them on such short notice was in an old tavern that had been converted into a bed and breakfast.

There was a shortage of reading material in the room, so the husband thumbed his bleary-eyed way through a travel brochure as he waited for his wife to complete her ritual nightly ablutions.

Besides the sea and the scenery, the principal local claim to fame was being home to the ghost of a bloodthirsty pirate.

A garish illustration depicted the buccaneer as a peg-legged privateer wielding a hook dripping with gore as he stood gloating over the body of an eviscerated sailor. The legend proclaimed that the nearly three-century old spirit of the dead pirate returned from time to time to claim fresh victims. His most recent atrocity had occurred within the living memory of the local gentry.

The tourist congratulated himself for not being superstitious. Otherwise, he'd have had to sleep with one eye open.

His spouse finished washing up and came to bed.

The couple slept soundly. The next morning, they awoke to discover the wife's diamond ring was missing from the bedside table where she'd put it. A quick search of their room failed to turn up the missing jewellery.

"This brochure says there are some mischievous ghosts residing here who like to go through visitors' luggage," the husband mentioned.

"Let me see," his wife said. She flipped through the pages, stopping to read a passage here and there. Finally, she nodded her head. "It also says there are some malevolent ghosts who only show up when they're summoned. Specifically, they can be called on to materialise by saying their names out loud three times. As a precaution, no names are listed. Not even nicknames. What a crock."

"If you say so. What now, Vera?"

"Call the police, Reggie, and don't settle for the village bobby—or whatever he's called—either. Talk to somebody with some rank."

Reginald did as he was told. He picked up his mobile phone and keyed in 1-1-2.

"Police... Hello, Inspector... Oh, you're *not* an inspector. May I speak to one, please?"

He cupped his hand over the phone.

"There's no inspector available. What should I do?"

"Tell them never mind. I just found my ring. It was under the pillow—how it got there, I'll never know."

Having worked up an appetite, they decided they should go downstairs and get some breakfast.

When the couple stepped out into the hallway, however, they were nearly bowled over by a running man. Without an apology, and without slowing down, the terrified man yelled at them, "Run for your lives! Some bloomin' idjit just conjured up the *Inn Spectre*!"

First published in *Daily Frights 2012*, Pill Hill Press, 2012

THE BLADE OF GUDRIN

By James Dorr

"No, I'm…I'm *not* a thief," Sarai protested. She looked up at the man who'd confronted her, seeing a smile crease his wind-beaten face—a smile that she, if she weren't still so frightened, might have considered an offer of friendship.

"I'm not of the city guard, milady," the man replied. "The reason I ask is that you are veiled, as if from the south. Perhaps you are one who worships the Black Stone—or else hiding something? I also see that you carry steel…"

She placed her hand carefully on her hip. "A simple desert knife," she said. "I've come from a caravan outside the city."

"Very few caravans seek out Bukhara these days, milady. I mean you no harm, but I would ask to see the blade of that knife more closely."

She looked around her, frantically hoping to find some escape, but the street she stood in was walled on both sides, and unlike the bazaar of the night before, its gates were shut to her. Besides, she realised, the man *did* look friendly. What choice did she have but to give him her trust?

"The caravan, actually, is at some distance," she said as she passed the knife, hilt forward, into the man's hand. She watched as he inspected its curved blade, first one side and then the other, then gave it back to her.

"What kind of knife is this?"

"Among my people, it's called a *janbiya*—as I said, simply a desert knife."

The man looked in her eyes, as if searching for something, then nodded and motioned to her to follow him. Sarai shrugged—what else could she do? She'd already wandered the maze-like city for hours that morning, getting more and more hopelessly lost as the dull copper sun rose up toward its zenith. She needed food and a place to rest so, nodding meekly in return, she let him lead her.

At last, they came to a secluded courtyard and, opening a door that stood across from its small, walled fountain, the man led her into a dimly lit inn. He paused for a few whispered words with the innkeeper, then motioned her into a curtained alcove.

Once they were seated, he reached to her veil. "Milady," he said when she twisted her head away from his hand, "I don't think you wear that for reasons of worship. It's best that you don't in any event since foreign religions aren't well received here."

Sarai nodded again. As a desert woman, she wore the veil for protection from the wind and sand, but in the city, she'd already been seen without it once when she'd hailed the gate the previous evening. The soldiers had drawn back as if, somehow, they'd *recognised* her, and once she was inside, she'd pinned it back up and ran, her long cloak flapping behind her, until she'd lost herself in the crowd of the city's bazaar. Now she removed it a second time with her own hands and, feeling the sharpness of terror return, she saw that this man drew back from her as well.

"I-I didn't lie, sir," she stammered. He *had* said before that he wouldn't harm her. "I did come here from a caravan, but one that's camped nearly four days to the west. I-I ran away from…"

The man again seemed to search her eyes closely.

"M-my name is Sarai. I ran away from the husband my father had chosen for me—a cruel husband. A powerful chief who my father feared, and who had me beaten, without any cause for it on my own part, and threatened to kill me. I…"

"I see," the man said. "I had to be sure, though, that you weren't the person some said you might be. You can call me Tel." He softened his voice and his smile returned, but only a half smile. "The knife you carry is much like one called the Blade of Gudrin, except the one she wields has blood-red characters etched in its steel.

And your face—I'd heard rumours that Gudrin was seen at the gates of the city yesterday evening, possibly going among her subjects as she sometimes does when she plans new evil, yet others had said she was still in her palace. Your face, too, except that your eyes aren't so hard, is much like Gudrin's."

"G-Gudrin the Blessed? I-I heard that name spoken by one of the soldiers…"

"Gudrin the Blessed, as she calls herself—yes. Gudrin the Good. Gudrin the Goddess. Queen of Bukhara. Gudrin, as others say when her guards and her priests can't hear them, the Ultimate Corrupter of People. In the right light, you could pass for her, Sarai."

"I…?"

"Don't say anything more for now, Sarai. I'm going to leave you, but just for a few hours. I've already given the innkeeper orders to bring you food—I know by the way you looked when we came in that you must be hungry. After you've eaten, he'll show you a place where you can sleep safely. Then, when I've come back, it will be time to talk."

****

"Sarai," a voice said.

She blinked and saw cushions strewn around her. Then she remembered—the inn's back room. She looked up at the man who'd whispered and saw it was Tel with a scroll in his hands.

"Sarai," he said again as he carefully unrolled the parchment. "This is a drawing of Gudrin's palace. I want you to memorise its features—its halls and its chambers—and then I'll be back with some other men who'll want to meet you."

She nodded, wondering how long she'd slept, then sat up and took the scroll into her own hands. She looked at it carefully even though she couldn't help thinking, as Tel turned to leave her, that he was younger than her husband and, while a large man, he had the appearance of being gentle. She shuddered at the thought of her husband—the hatred and fear—the memory of her final decision, as she'd searched for food and extra skins to be filled with water, to risk death alone in a storm in the desert than stay another night in his tent. She reached to her knife and felt its hilt at her side where it should be—if Tel had had her betrayal in mind, the thought came to her, he surely wouldn't have left it with her.

In any event, she reminded herself she had little choice. She knew no one else in this isolated oasis city. She smoothed the scroll out again on the floor next to the lamp Tel had left at her side and began to memorise its details.

Perhaps an hour later she heard a scratching sound at the door, then Tel's voice again, asking for entrance. She called out an answer and watched as it opened and Tel strode in with three other men.

She saw the most richly dressed of them nod as the four took cushions and seated themselves in a circle around her.

By instinct, she reached to her knife again, then drew her hand back.

"Sarai," Tel said, "go ahead and draw it. These men are friends, but just as I needed to before, they'll want to have a look at its blade."

She did as he asked and handed it to the richly dressed man who looked at it closely, then held it up so the others could see. He nodded again, then handed it back, whispering something to Tel as he did so.

"Sarai," Tel said, "this man to my right used to be a merchant. He still gets by, as I think you can see by the robes he's wearing, despite the fact that, when Gudrin first came to Bukhara, she had his entire stock of goods confiscated. This one to my left is a guard at the palace—his brother was killed—and the one behind you saw his son die because, when he was sick, Gudrin's taxes had left too little to pay for a doctor. And you, Sarai, have little reason to love Gudrin either because, when reports of you gain her attention, it's not very likely she'll want you to live…"

"B-but what can I do? I-I can't change my features…"

"What you can do is wear your veil one more night for us," the merchant broke in. "You have memorised the plans of the palace? What you must do is go there this evening, before the midnight change of the guards. The one who is with us will be on duty at the side gate and will pass you in. Then you must hide yourself inside the palace until the other attendants are sleeping. Can you do that, Sarai?"

She nodded slowly, remembering how when the bazaar closed the night before, she'd concealed herself in the dust and filth of Bukhara's alleys until the morning, and even for several hours after that had wandered unnoticed until Tel had found her.

"Good," said the merchant. "Now, once you're sure that it's safe to do so, you will have to seek out Gudrin's bedchamber. Inside you must look for a knife that resembles yours and…"

"B-but if she's a goddess, would she have to sleep like other people? I mean, I could get as far as her chamber, but once I've reached it…"

"Sarai," the one that Tel had said was

a guard interrupted. "Gudrin is a goddess, yes, but her spirit inhabits a woman's body. She may sleep lightly—rumours of the palace have it that, because of the evil she's done, she's disturbed by dreams—but she <u>will</u> be sleeping. In any event, all you must do is take her knife and put yours in its sheath in its place."

"You see, Sarai," the merchant added, "the goddess' protection resides in that knife—in the words that are etched in Gudrin's Blade. Once it's taken from her— and with yours in its sheath to replace it, unless she has reason to draw it out, she's not even likely to realise its loss—it will then be possible for us and the others who've suffered with us to take back the city."

"I-I still don't understand," Sarai protested. "I-I mean, to go into a goddess' bedchamber…"

"An ordinary woman's, Sarai, without her knife at her side to protect her," Tel said softly. "That's why Bukhara depends on you—depends on your resemblance to Gudrin to let you get out of the palace safely and bring it to us so we can destroy it." His voice dropped further. "It's why I depend on you as well, Sarai."

Sarai gazed for several minutes at the thinly carpeted floor, then looked up again into Tel's eyes. She saw sorrow and pain. "Tel," she whispered, "you've said the merchant lost his business because of Gudrin. The palace guard saw his brother killed, and your other friend blames her for the loss of his son to an illness. But what is your reason for hating the goddess?"

"My own wife, Sarai, resembled her too. Not as closely as you resemble her, but enough that Gudrin took notice. My wife was tortured before she died, and her body, instead of being buried, was given over to Gudrin's priests to use for their pleasure…"

***

Sarai huddled behind a curtain as yet another servant passed by. It had been nearly a half hour since the last one, however, and this one carried a candle with him, as if on the way to his own bedchamber. Soon, she thought. All too soon it would be time to use what she'd learned of the palace to seek the goddess.

She thought back to the hours with Tel, after the other men had left them, making sure she'd memorised the scroll he'd brought to her. Then, well after darkness, he'd taken her to the city's main square and showed her the gate she'd use to gain entrance, as well as the route she'd have to take, after, to where he and his friends would be waiting. And then he'd kissed her, not in the rough way her husband used women, but in a softer, more gentle way that caused her to raise her veil herself when she parted her lips to his in return.

She thought of the kiss as she counted the minutes—she knew well how to estimate time as well as keep silent as she waited. Twenty, thirty, forty more passed before she finally crept out from the curtain, letting her veil drop, so if she were seen now, she might be mistaken for the goddess on some night errand. She kept to the left wall of the passageway, in near darkness, counting her paces, counting the turns. At last, she came up to what her hands told her was a deeply carved wooden door.

She felt the carvings, comparing them in her mind to a sketch that had been on the parchment, then eased the door open enough to slip through. She found herself in a large anteroom, dimly lit by the moon through its windows. Around her she saw the goddess' treasures, her tables and cushions and gilded jewel chests, her gowns and accoutrements ready for use. And alone in a corner, next to the arch that led further inside, she saw a gold peg and a belt that hung from it.

Attached to the belt she could see a curved sheath, much like the one she wore at her own hip. Except that this sheath was encrusted with gemstones.

She crossed the room, not with the silence of a thief, but with the wary kind of quietness of one who had been raised a desert tribeswoman. She reached for the sheath—then realised, with an audible gasp, that it was empty.

She turned and slipped, her foot catching under a bench, and froze as the near archway blazed into brightness.

"So," the voice of a woman whispered, "the rumours my soldiers brought me were true. A wench who came through the gates of my city, only last night, veiling herself to conceal <u>my</u> features."

Sarai stepped backward, freeing her foot as she did so, and watched as Gudrin strode into the room with a lamp in her hand. She backed away again, another step toward the outer door as the goddess reached up and fastened the light to a hanging bracket, then froze a second time when she saw a flash of red.

"Might I presume that you came for my pretty—the Blade of Gudrin?" the thinly night-robed goddess taunted. "I trust you didn't think I was so foolish not to keep it safe under my pillow."

Sarai eased her cloak off her shoulders, keeping her eyes on the red-etched knife the goddess now held. She backed again, this time into a crouched position, and wrapped the cloak loosely around her left forearm.

"But, if you've come all this way for my bauble," the goddess continued, her voice taking on a low, soothing tone, "I think you should have it." She took a step forward, holding the knife out in front of her chest, weaving it slowly from side to side in a serpentine motion. She took another step, closing the distance, when Sarai leaped sideways, her own knife flashing.

Sarai's blade struck first, opening a gash on the goddess' left shoulder. Desert fighting—she crouched down again, raising her cloaked arm to ward off Gudrin's expected return blow, pulling her own knife back close to her belly.

But Gudrin just turned to face Sarai again. "You think to hurt me?" the goddess purred. Sarai watched, continuing to circle, as her opponent's wound drew itself closed, the skin smoothing over—as Gudrin took another step forward. A smaller step this time.

Sarai thrust again, this time feinting to Gudrin's midsection, then whipped her point upward to slash at the goddess' unguarded face. She laid a cheek open, exposing the bone. She saw the goddess flinch, heard a sharp indrawing of breath, then watched as the red line, just like the shoulder wound before it, completed its healing in front of her eyes.

"You'd try again, wench?" This time

the goddess' voice no longer purred. "Did you not know that I am protected from such filth as you? But enough of this playing."

The goddess moved quickly, thrusting downward as Sarai countered, deflecting the blade with her cloaked left fist. *The goddess feels pain*, she thought as she parried a second attack, then dodged to her right. *And she doesn't fight as we do in the desert—she holds her blade forward...*

Sarai dodged again, then heard the sound of footsteps in the hallway outside. "My priests approach, carrion," the goddess said. "But first, <u>my</u> pleasure..."

Sarai thought quickly. She holds her blade forward, away from her body—what was it that the merchant had told her? She waited this time for the goddess' next thrust, then, twisting sideways, letting her cloak take the force of the blow, she brought her own blade down on Gudrin's wrist.

The goddess' knife dropped—and Sarai, flinging her cloak in front of her, dropped to the floor too. Gudrin's protection, the merchant had told her, resided in the words etched in her weapon's steel. She came up with the blade in her right hand, shifting her own knife into her left, and staggered backward just as the door to the chamber burst open.

"Malzar! Valderon! Seize the wench quickly," Gudrin screamed. The priests stood in the doorway, staring, as Sarai felt a rush of…enjoyment…course through her body. She shook the feeling off, backing farther as she, too, stared at the goddess' wrist. At the blood that continued to flow from its wound onto the richly carpeted floor.

"Do you hear me, Malzar?"

The more ornately robed of the priests nodded and took a step forward. He struck Gudrin's face, then signalled the other to seize her shoulders. Together they twisted the now mute woman around until all three faced Sarai.

"We wait for your orders, Blessed Goddess," the first priest said quietly. Sarai crouched, feeling the heft of the knife in her hand—again feeling pleasure—then realised the priest was addressing her.

She who held the Blade of Gudrin.

She licked her lips—the words came

out almost before she'd formed them. "Hold the bitch for me, just as you are doing now, Malzar."

She smiled and came forward with slow, mincing steps, giving herself to the pleasure's bidding, then thrust her knife upward, desert fashion, into the soft flesh beneath Gudrin's rib cage. She twisted the curved blade and ripped it higher, exulting in the feel of hot blood on her hands and arms, until the hilt had become so slippery she couldn't continue.

"Now," she sighed, pulling the blade out, wiping it clean on the dead woman's hair, "you may leave me, Malzar. You also, Valderon—take the corpse for whatever use you and your fellows may have—but come back to me again in my chambers after the sun's rise."

She watched as the priests bowed their dismissal, then turned to the peg by the arched inner door. She reached for the belt there and placed it around her, sliding the blade in the sheath that hung from it. She thought she'd seen the chief priest, Malzar, wink when they'd left her, but it didn't matter. She knew she now resembled the old Gudrin quite well enough for the rest of her people.

She knew Gudrin's secret—the power of Gudrin was not in a mere knife. She left the chamber and strode down the darkened, maze-like halls to the gates of her palace, feeling the goddess' spirit within her, the goddess' own joy as she planned the betrayal of Tel and the others who'd sought to use her to gain their own power. And after that…yes. She licked her lips in anticipation.

And after that she would raise an army among the people of Bukhara. An army whose first task would be to conquer the husband of Sarai, the desert woman—the woman who had become <u>herself</u> the Blade of Gudrin.

First published in *Spring 1993*, Space and Time Magazine, 1993

THE HAND OF THE QUEEN

By Georgia Megan

The fragile shield of ice-kissed air slammed into place around the army a mere second before the firebomb shook the foundation of the earth. I gritted my teeth against the impact, even as I felt the ice splinter like glass when the fire crackled against it. The power rushed from me moments later, the icy wind forcing back the encroaching flames. Too fast; my power was depleting too fast.

My face was slick with sweat, my breath ragged. I glared up at the sun, still stubbornly holding on to daylight, and wished for it to sink already. The sun was just one more weapon against us.

Glancing to my left and right, I saw that even the strongest of our wielders weren't much better off. My grip tightened on the familiar steel in my right hand. The battle pitted magic against magic, but soon enough, only the clang of steel against steel would echo across the devastated Blood Peninsula; the sound interspersed with the pleas of the fallen.

My left hand gripped a worn piece of parchment. The final orders from the queen to her most trusted legion.

The Golden Hand has taken up refuge in the abandoned village on the northern borders. Deal with them by any means necessary. Protect this kingdom. Rid us of this blight. You march at dawn.

Red sand crunched underfoot as my second and third approached me, taking up flanking positions on both sides as I surveyed the battle. Slipping the parchment into edge of my armour, I signalled for the remaining wielders to resurrect the ice-shield, before inclining my head to Tarren, my second.

Tarren's words were clipped, his

report brief. "General, the Golden Hand is holding strong against our attacks." I glanced sideways at Tarren to see his jaw was clenched.

"How? The last time they faced us on the battlefield, it was over within minutes."

Tarren heard the commanding question in my tone. I didn't want excuses; I wanted answers.

"I have the spies looking into it. It seems the Hand have acquired either a new weapon or means of defence."

"You think?" I muttered.

We all watched as a large fireball erupted from the horizon and soared straight towards our defensive line. The ground shook, and the shield splintered as the fire exploded right in front of us. My soldiers staggered ever so slightly and Juba, my third, called for them to keep formation.

In quick succession, multiple blasts of fire lit up the blood red dirt before us. They joined to form one hot, deadly wave that swept towards us, rising higher and higher. Our shield cracked some more, as if it could sense it was about to be decimated.

"Soldiers! Fall back. Wielders, with me." I marched forward until I stood at the head of the remaining group. The sun was dropping low in the sky; it made the whole plain look like it was on fire.

"The Hand are going to crash that wave down on us. If we don't act, give it everything we've got, it will smash through the shield and straight onto your comrades.

Gather all your strength and power. We don't have *time* to be tired."

As one they focussed, and as one they began to reinforce and patch up the ice-shield. I reached inside me, into that almost empty magic reserve, and channelled what I could into helping them.

On my best day, my shield was impenetrable. Today was not my best day. Every nerve, muscle and bone ached. My magic was a whisper of what it should be.

As the wave swept closer, tendrils licking at the shield, I heard Tarren commanding the soldiers to brace for a hard impact. Almost everyone else had retreated into safer territory. Tarren knew just as I did; that this peninsula was about to be stained with blood and steel, and that we needed strong, living soldiers to even have a chance at winning this.

The Hand's power must have indeed grown. Their wielders' control over magic definitely had, because the wave had slowed. And the slower it was, the larger it seemed to be getting. It seemed they weren't taking any chances that we would escape destruction.

The sun slipped below the horizon, yet the world continued to grow hotter and brighter. Sheathing my sword, I ran forward until I was inches from the barrier of the shield. A wisp of ice in the air flowed over me, followed by a sense of calm.

"General!" I heard cries from behind me, the voices repeating my title over and over again in alarm.

I reached a hand out behind me to halt any advances. I heard Tarren's voice next.

"Hold your positions, wielders. Just because the General is being an idiot doesn't mean we want everyone to follow suit."

I cracked a small smile and made a vulgar gesture over my shoulder as I placed my left-hand flush against the shield. The wave of flame was almost upon us. It blocked out everything around us, as if to cry out: 'Look at this great wall of death coming to get you. *You cannot escape this.*'

But blocking out everything was exactly what I needed, so I closed my eyes. Ice flowed from my fingertips, reinforcing the shield over and over. Every drop of my power dedicated to protecting my army. A second later, a light flashed bright behind my eyelids, and then the world went dark.

***

"Etri!" Tarren's voice was sharp, too loud against my sensitive ears. "Get up, you self-sacrificing asshole."

My throat felt like it was lined with shards of glass as I swallowed and let Tarren to roll me over. Red dust swirled in my vision as I blinked once, twice. Tarren's face came into focus through the haze. His head haloed by the last pink rays of sunset.

"What happened?" I coughed out, blood and dust spattering the sand as I emptied my lungs. Tarren roughly patted me on the back. By the sound of him grinding his teeth, it was half in sympathy, half him wanting to wallop me.

"You placed yourself right in front of a wave of magical fire. What do you *think* happened?"

I pushed myself up until Tarren took pity on me, hooking a hand under my elbow and hoisting me to my feet. Blood and sand had mixed together on my skin, giving the impression that every inch of me was bleeding. I could feel a gash in my left arm, and my head throbbed. I reached up to my hair and found it matted with blood. Wonderful. At least I was bound to intimidate the poor souls I encountered on the battlefield.

I took a step forward and realised I was a hundred feet from the front line, a hundred feet from my soldiers who were now facing an advancing group of the

Golden Hand. No whisper of fire or ice in the air. Only steel against steel, fighter against fighter.

"Didn't the shield hold?" I asked, sombrely observing the craters of flame that dotted the field where my army had been holding the line.

Tarren unsheathed his sword, prompting me to pull myself together and do the same. His eyes were tracking something far in the distance. Juba's head bobbed in and out of vision as she organised the troops into formation.

I knew from the set of Tarren's jaw that we couldn't dawdle much longer. I was itching to join the fight, as much as he was itching to draw closer to his lover.

"The shield held enough to protect us,

but I think your power reacted instinctively." He gave me a funny look as we quickly traversed the terrain to catch up with the advancing soldiers. "You reinforced the shield above us, by removing a lot of the protection right in front of you. You somehow manipulated the shield until we were encased in a secondary tight layer of ice. We were stuck. We couldn't get you, couldn't break through. All that stood between you and death was a flimsy remainder of the wielders' magic."

I cringed. Tarren and Juba were both loyal to the very end. They would put their life above mine a million times over to avoid any harm coming to me, so it must have been torture—to watch, not only their

General, but one of their oldest friends, stand alone and face down an unbelievable feat of magic. If the roles had been reversed, I would have torn down the world to protect them.

"The wielders exploded the ice-shield the second the fire hit, managing to push a lot of the frontal force back. It still crashed down on us, but the shield held long enough for most of the fire to dissolve, before the dome fell away and we scattered. You got blown all the way back here from the sheer force of it all. I've been trying to wake you up for fifteen minutes."

Soldiers parted as we stepped up behind them, allowing us to move swiftly through the ranks. Whispers followed our every step. It seemed my sacrifice and survival had re-motivated the soldiers into believing we could live to see another day. Hadn't been my original plan, but I'd take it.

We reached Juba, and I felt Tarren relax beside me as he confirmed she was still in one piece. "General," she acknowledged with a sharp nod. "Good to see you up and about. Wasn't really the best time for you to take a power nap." Juba grinned and indicated towards the encroaching resistance fighters. "Orders?"

"Let our magic replenish itself. Go steel on steel and let's gain some territory back. It'll get too dark for them to see anything soon; those fires won't last for long."

Tarren and Juba both nodded, heading

off to the army's flanks to relay the orders to all. True enough, without the wave of fire to light up the peninsula, darkness was beginning to take control. All of my soldiers had heightened senses, and I could tell their eyes were adjusting to the darkness from the way their irises began to give off a luminescent glow, the distinctive light revealing their ice-wielder nature.

We were creatures born of cold, dark magic. The ice was our lifeblood, the darkness our home.

On whispered signals and pure instinct, the soldiers broke off into numerous small stealth units. Easier to sneak across the territory and get into the Golden Hand's terrain.

It was our time now, the time of ice

and darkness. With the sun having finally fallen below the horizon, the fire-wielders were nearly powerless. They had waited on the battlefield too long, been arrogant in their last push for power, and now they would live—or die—to regret it.

The last of the fires glowed as mere embers as the Hand began to fall. Hushed cries of help and death, and almost silent thumps as my army dispatched fighter after fighter.

This was why the queen sent us. There was a reason we were dubbed the Nightcrawler legion. We had taken down many a kingdom, dispatching soldiers and royals alike, by moving as swift and silently as the darkness itself. No one saw us coming until we were on top of them.

Which is why this battle didn't sit right with me. What still grated on my nerves was why the queen had sent us in as the frontline so quickly, when it was still daylight and everyone knew that the fire-wielders would be more powerful. We weren't a huge legion, yet I had already lost a few good soldiers, purely from fighting without the cover of darkness and having travelled a long way to get here. If I didn't know any better, I would say we had been set up to fail.

But I couldn't think about that now.

I slipped like smoke in-between my soldiers, heading for the Golden Hand's front line, and the commander cowering just behind it. Juba and Tarren had slotted into position alongside me and swiftly took down any foot soldiers I'd not bothered to dispatch.

And there she was. The commander of the enemy, weak and terrified and ever so vulnerable. She could have run. *Should* have run. But she'd stayed to fight us, as inevitable as such an outcome would be.

My sword was at the commander's throat before she'd even managed to grip the handle of her own.

She shook violently as I called for a ceasefire, hoping she'd repeat my orders when facing the threat of death. But she didn't even need to. I knew what her remaining soldiers would decide to do seconds before they turned and ran like cowards. The broken men and women ran for the horizon.

"Bastards," muttered the commander, still shaking in my grip. I felt a pang of sympathy for the young leader. A moment of crisis, and every single one of her soldiers had fled rather than stay with her. But I couldn't afford to be soft.

"Restrain her," I yelled, shoving her into my closest soldiers. The commander struggled as her hands and feet were bound and she was gagged and thrown to the floor, red dust shimmering in the moonlight and the luminescent glow of our eyes.

"General," reported a soldier. "The rest of the Hand have fled back to their base in the village a mile to the north. Captain Tarren was right: they do have advanced weaponry in their arsenal." The young soldier's face looked scared, almost as if I was going to shoot the messenger. That had only happened once…okay, *twice*.

"Show me." The soldier nodded and turned on her heel, leading me to some tents and crates left behind by the Hand. We hadn't noticed them in our previous scouting, and I now realised why Tarren had been unable to determine what sort of weapon the Hand possessed.

Behind the crates and tents, hidden among some large clusters of rock, was the mysterious weapon we had been seeking. It was built into the stone itself. No wonder we hadn't spotted it.

As we approached, Juba's steps faltered slightly. Her face scrunching up as she frowned at the mechanisms with her tongue between her teeth.

"Do you know what it is?" I asked, rounding the rock to stand beside her, behind the weapon. It looked to me like some sort of launcher. Probably how they were able to launch fireballs with such power and accuracy.

My eyes scanned every inch of metal that was welded together to create the structure, but I couldn't see a power source anywhere. None of the Hand were strong fire-wielders. How did they even fuel a weapon of this magnitude?

"I don't like this." Juba mumbled, glancing apprehensively at the tied-up commander. "I don't like this one bit." I caught her wrist.

"What are you thinking?"

"That I hope I'm wrong." Her eyes

saddened for a second before becoming hard as stone once again. Juba tugged her wrist out of my grasp and strode until she was staring down at the commander's constrained body.

With a flicker of speed, I moved to stand next to her, arms crossed and trying to steel myself for what was about to be revealed. Something had unsettled one of the most hardened and ruthless warriors I knew.

"Where did you get it?" asked Juba, her voice ice cold and unforgiving.

The commander started to laugh, which quickly turned into a choking cough as she breathed in blood and dust. I nodded to the soldiers guarding her and they tugged her roughly to her feet.

"Answer the question." My tone was dark and even as I levelled my gaze on the commander. Her eyes widened as mine flashed, but her cocky grin remained.

"Or you'll do what? You're already going to kill me. The Nightcrawlers never leave any survivors."

Slowly, so she could hear the slide of my knife against its sheath, I pulled out my favourite blade. The slightly curved tip, glimmering gently in the low moonlight.

"Or *else*, I start slicing."

I stepped forward and she flinched.

"You were right when you said we don't leave anyone alive," I added. "Sometimes, though, we take our time with the deaths." My soldiers started grinning as I pressed the blade against her throat. "And on even rarer occasions, we leave one person alive; just long enough to pass on the legend of the Nightcrawlers. How else do you think rumours get around when we leave no one alive?"

She visibly gulped.

"So, you can either live… mostly. Or die. Slowly."

I handed the knife to one of my soldiers and stepped back.

"Your choice, Commander." I turned my back and started towards the tents, nodding at Juba to follow me. "Let us know when she is ready to talk." I added.

The commander's screams echoed in every footstep as we left her to her fate.

****

Tarren had ordered for the Hand's

tents to be taken stock of and made fit for our use. No fires had been lit. While the darkness was still present, we held the advantage. The Golden Hand knew where we were, but without fire or some other form of light, they wouldn't see an attack until it was right on top of them.

I marched into the main tent and dismissed everyone but Tarren and Juba. "Rotation of patrols and inventory," I directed at the nearest soldier.

My orders were received, and we were soon alone. "Tell me what you know, now."

Juba sighed. "Or what, you'll threaten me with your big shiny knife?" She flopped down into the nearest chair and I rolled my eyes.

"Juba," I said, my voice firm. "I know there's something you're not telling me, and it's something big. You don't scare easily. As your General, consider it an order."

Her eyes narrowed, but she started to speak regardless. I didn't miss the defensive position Tarren took up next to her chair.

"I've seen that device before," Juba said. "But I can't for the life of me figure out how it ended up on this battlefield and with the Golden Hand. There is only one in existence, at least as far as I knew."

"What does it do?"

"It's essentially a conduit for wielders. A way for them to strengthen their power without draining it: the machine multiplies it for you and lets you increase accuracy and power of shots. You can create anything. You're not limited by your own skills…if you can think it, you can wield it using the machine."

I didn't think I was breathing. "And where did they get it?" My jaw was clenched so tight, the words were barely distinguishable.

"Etri, I hope I am wrong."

"Where, Juba?"

She sighed, "The queen. It is the queen's latest creation."

My fist slammed down on the makeshift table before I could even think. The wood froze and splintered into fragments of ice under my hand. "They stole from our queen? From our kingdom?"

Both Juba and Tarren held their tongues, as they often did when I started to break things. Most likely because I had once broken one of their noses when they interrupted me during a rage.

"The Hand has just signed their own final death sentence," I muttered.

"We will get them," Tarren said. "They've fled to the abandoned village to the north. It's a ghost settlement, General, with no one there but the Hand's soldiers. I scouted it personally to confirm. We can wipe them out."

I nodded slowly, digesting what we had learnt and what was to happen next. What <u>had</u> to happen.

"General?" A soldier popped his head through the tent flap and I lifted my gaze.

To his credit, he didn't flinch at the molten ice that was brewing behind my eyes. "She wants to talk."

The temperature dropped as I let out an icy breath, my power refilling. What horrible timing for the commander.

My footsteps were quick as I made my way back to the prisoner, my second and third hot on my heels.

I found the commander dripping with blood, her head wobbling and primarily supported by the strength of my soldiers flanking her. A satisfied smile appeared on my face.

"How did you come to be in possession of such a weapon?"

Tarren hid his snort with a cough at my attempt to be civil to the woman I was itching to kill.

"The queen," The commander mumbled, blood gurgling and slurring her speech. My hands balled into icy fists.

"How did you get hold of the weapon? Did you steal it?" asked Tarren, his voice as cold as my heart.

The commander laughed, choking on more blood. "The queen."

I gritted my teeth and poured all my remaining self-control into not killing her.

"Answer the damn question!" Juba commanded, striding forwards and punching the commander straight in the face. Her head snapped back with a satisfying crunch, but her ridiculous laughter continued.

"The queen." The commander started

to chant the words over and over. She stared right into my eyes, that psychotic bloody grin still on her face as I reached inside her and froze her heart.

I was already halfway back to the tent as I heard her body thump lifeless and cold onto the red sand.

I changed destinations mid-stride and headed towards the weapon. The darkness still covered us; we had time to come up with another assault and finish the rebels. I didn't need to get caught up in how and why this weapon was sitting here, somehow being used by my enemies.

"Etri?" I turned to find Tarren watching me like I was about to explode. "What are you thinking?"

I ran my finger along the edge of the

metal of the device, and it seemed to purr to life in response. What a weapon.

Something like this had been suggested in a council meeting a long time ago. The idea had been shot down at the time, as it had been unanimously agreed that no one person should be able to wield such power. It created much more possibility for further rebellion, even from within our own ranks. Yet now here it was. As solid and dangerous as the sword strapped to my hip, as the ice that flowed in my veins.

"You said the village was abandoned except for the Golden Hand. You're sure?"

I glanced at my second, but Tarren didn't even hesitate. "Yes, General."

I nod slowly. "The queen sent us to

dispatch the Hand. She told us they would be here at this spot. Which they were."

I glanced up at Tarren.

"Let's use that," Tarren said, nodding at the device, "and end this. We still have the darkness on our side," he finished.

I shook my head. "We don't even need it." My hand rested against the metal of the weapon and a living flame of ice appeared in my other hand, luminescent in the light of our eyes. Darkness didn't matter when with one strike, I could wipe out the Hand for good.

***

The decision of who should manipulate the weapon was obvious. Which meant Tarren and Juba had to coordinate the troops and let me know when to strike. With the amount of power I felt emanating from the device, I had no guarantee I would have control over myself or my magic. I certainly couldn't command an army at the same time.

I scanned the horizon. We would end this once and for all. For the people in this kingdom, for my queen. That was what the Nightcrawlers were made for: dispatch the enemies, avenge those who had been wronged. Leave no survivors.

We managed to reposition the weapon to face towards the village and I moved in behind it, my soldiers all watching with a glimmer of both excitement and apprehension.

Tarren had decided on the centre square as the best target. I was to create a ball of ice that I would direct right to the square, and then along with the wielders, we would detonate it and decimate the village. The strength of the weapon and our combined power meant we knew the outcome even before firing.

This war would end tonight.

I closed my eyes and let my power leak into the machine. A light glowed in front of my eyelids, and a refreshing air washed over me. I knew without looking that the ice-weapon was bigger and scarier than anything I had ever created.

I couldn't hear my soldiers; I couldn't even open my eyes. Yet I didn't need to. The machine was seeing for me, moving for me. Adjusting my aim and the strength of the ice by pure thought. Somewhere through the haze of power I heard Tarren shout for me to fire; and suddenly the machine let me go, just as it launched our creation into the air.

It looked like the moon was about to fall on the village, a huge white sphere of beauty and death. As it fell to the earth, I let my eyes relax. Almost unbidden, my enhanced vision zoomed in and settled on the square as a movement caught my eye.

Stumbling forward, I tried to call for a ceasefire, but it was too late.

Far too late.

The ice seemed to lick the rooftops of the village as my zoomed-in vision landed on a Hand member, clutching a crying little boy in their arms. A terrified child clutching a toy and screaming, surrounded by a flurry of other Hand members and captured civilians.

Not a ghost village at all, despite what Tarren had sworn to me. There were members of this kingdom in that village. Those helpless individuals whom I had sworn to protect. I was not their salvation, but rather their damnation.

My knees gave way as everything exploded, and I watched the light leave the little boy's eyes forever.

ELSPETH

By Rich Rurshell

The gunfire in the tiny bedroom was deafening. But just as suddenly as it had begun, it ended. Elspeth cowered beneath her bed, silent.

"Move out."

Elspeth peered from beneath the bed to

see several pairs of booted feet leaving her room. Why hadn't her parents come to warn her? They had said they would warn her if the soldiers came to their village. They said they would all hide together.

The soldiers shouted in the room beneath her, but she could not hear her parents. Maybe they hid without her. She remained still and listened to the footsteps of the soldiers, and the vehicle noises and shouting from outside. After a few minutes, the noises from downstairs ceased, and Elspeth could only hear the soldiers outside. She could hear gunfire elsewhere, possibly a scream, she wasn't sure. She was just glad they hadn't found her.

"You can come out now."

Elspeth dared not even breathe. That

voice wasn't like any voice she had ever heard. Slowly, she turned to where the voice had come from. Instead of the booted feet she had expected, there stood two black hooves. What little of the legs Elspeth could see was covered in coarse, black hair.

"I'm not going to hurt you."

Elspeth wondered why there was a horse in her bedroom. One that can talk. Since it knew she was there, she slid out from under the bed.

It wasn't a horse.

Standing before Elspeth was a tall figure, with great, black, leathery wings folded behind its back. Staring at her were two piercing, yellow eyes that sat above a mouth full of pointed teeth. A pair of small horns on the creature's forehead curled back over the top of its head. It took a step towards her, offering a large hand to help her up. It spread its wings across her bedroom, creating a small corridor between itself and the wall which led to the window. As she took the hand and stood up, she noticed the large claws on each finger.

"We should leave. Through there." The monster nodded at the window. Despite the grotesque appearance of this creature, Elspeth did not feel at all threatened. In fact, after the terror of being awoken by gunfire, she now felt safe. She was no longer alone.

"It's too high. We'll fall," she replied. The monster grinned.

"No, we won't," it said, pointing to its

wings.

Elspeth walked over to the window and looked out. There didn't appear to be any soldiers nearby, but she could still hear gunfire somewhere.

"We're going to fly out?"

"We sure are. Are you ready?"

Elspeth opened the window and climbed up onto the ledge. She tried to take a last look at her room before they left, but the huge wings blocked her view. Before she could say anything else, the creature pushed her from the window, and she found herself wrapped in its arms, gliding over the front yard of her home. They flew out over her neighbour's garden and down the street. Further across the village, she could see the soldiers lining people up in the street. People she recognised. Before she could see why, the creature soared upwards. Elspeth looked up and saw the clouds above quickly approaching.

"Ready?" it said.

Elspeth laughed as they were engulfed and gasped as they popped out of the top of the cold, wet blanket of white. The creature dropped back down to the cloud, and its hooves landed softly on its surface.

"Make yourself comfortable. We've got quite the view, eh?" It set her down on the cloud, and Elspeth looked out across the blue sky. She could see other clouds, the bright sun which bathed them in warmth and light, and the crescent moon which was still just about visible in the morning sky. The creature sat down on the cloud, so Elspeth did the same.

"What's your name, little girl?"

"Elspeth."

"And how old are you, Elspeth?"

"I'm five."

"Hmmm..." The monster was silent for a moment, in thought.

"What's *your* name," asked Elspeth.

"Klor." He once again offered Elspeth his large hand, gently shaking her tiny hand. "It's a pleasure to make your acquaintance, Elspeth."

"How old are *you*, Klor?"

Klor laughed. "Very."

"What are you, Klor?"

"I'm just Klor... How do you like the view from here, Elspeth?"

"It's nice."

"I bet you've never seen the world from this height before."

"You're right. I haven't." Elspeth got up and ran over to the edge of the cloud. She looked down at the land far beneath her. "Everything looks so small."

"Yes, it does." Klor chuckled.

"Klor, can you help me find my parents? I don't want those soldiers to catch them."

"Sure. I don't know where they are right now. When I do, I'll take you to them. Until then, don't you want to have some fun?"

"What kind of fun?"

"That's up to you. What would be fun for you?"

Elspeth looked around. "Can we fly to

the moon, Klor?"

Klor laughed heartily. "The moon is a long way away, Elspeth." He stood up and joined Elspeth at the cloud's edge. "But I think I know how to get us there."

Elspeth cheered and jumped up and down. "Ready then?"

"I'm ready. Hold tight." Klor scooped up Elspeth into his arms, then leapt from the cloud. They glided through the sky, then Klor beat his wings, taking them higher and higher. Elspeth looked at the moon as they flew towards it. She noticed that some small wisps of cloud were forming a circle ahead of them. Slowly, the circle began to turn.

"What's that ring, Klor?"

"That's a portal. We're going to use it

to get to the moon."

"We're going to..."

A sudden flash of golden light to their left and a loud thunderclap interrupted Elspeth. She turned her head and saw a man in a white robe, with large, white, feathered wings hurtling towards them.

"HALT!" the man cried.

"Who is that?" asked Elspeth.

"I wouldn't worry too much about him at the moment," said Klor, as he and Elspeth flew into the portal.

***

Elspeth looked down onto the Earth from the night sky. She and Klor sat in a small crater on the moon's surface.

"Can we see my house from here?"

"I wouldn't think so. We're too high."

"Where is your house, Klor?"

"Elsewhere. Another place. Though, I don't spend much time there."

"Why? Don't you like it at home?"

"Actually, I love my home. It's not to everyone's taste, but there are many wonders to behold, just like in your world. Your mountains, your oceans, your forests. My home has a great black ocean that boils constantly. The roar of that ocean is breathtaking. There are tall, black mountains that spew lava and ash into the darkness. Such beauty can only be believed once you have seen it. But it is your forests that intrigue me. Nothing grows in my home. Only burns. You lived near the forests. How do you find them, Elspeth?"

"The forests are beautiful. Father

sometimes takes me out for walks in the early morning. We see deer, and rabbits, and squirrels." Elspeth turned to Klor. "When can we find my parents?"

Klor continued staring down at the land. "I'll help you find them once we are finished here."

"What do we need to do here?"

"You asked me if we could fly to the moon, so we did. I brought you here so you could experience the beauty of this world. Of your world. You are so young. So much you haven't seen. Do you like your world?"

"Of course I do. It's a beautiful world. I like all the mountains and the forests and the sea, but I love my mother and father more. Can't we go and get them and bring them here?"

"Hmmm...we'll see," answered Klor. He stroked his chin, whilst staring out into the nothing.

"Are you alright, Klor?" asked Elspeth, putting her small hand on Klor's arm. Klor turned to face her and smiled.

"No one has ever asked me that, Elspeth. I'm good, thank you. Content with my existence." He smiled. "Are you ready to go now?"

"Back to my home? To find my parents?"

Klor sighed. "Those aren't the same thing anymore, Elspeth. Things have changed. Changed a lot. The war in your land has changed everything for you. For a lot of people. But I swear to you I will help you find your parents wherever they may be."

"Great! Let's go then." Elspeth jumped up into Klor's arms, and he chuckled as he spread his wings and took off. "Bye, Moon," she shouted as a new portal opened in front of them.

"BYE, ELSPETH," the moon boomed back in reply. Klor chuckled again, and they flew into the portal.

***

Klor flew over mountain ranges, along the coastline, and over forests with Elspeth. They swooped down every now and then to get a closer look at some particularly beautiful scenery, and each time they did, Elspeth would giggle and cling tight to Klor. They did this until a clap of thunder and another flash of golden light drew their attention. Once again, the man in the white robe flew towards them.

"Klor?"

"Fear not, Elspeth. This is what we've been waiting for," said Klor as he descended to the ground. They gently landed in a forest clearing, and Klor put Elspeth down. The winged man landed in front of them a moment later. Elspeth wrapped her arms around Klor's leg, and he gently laid his hand on her head.

"Unhand her, demon," demanded the man.

"A little dramatic, Briathos."

"Do I know you, demon?"

"We've not met before. Klor is the name. I'm familiar with your work. Elspeth, this is Briathos. Briathos, Elspeth.

He's going to help us find your parents."

"Klor? I've heard your name. The angels say you are not a typical demon. But I find myself curious as to why you have taken the soul of this young girl. Elspeth you say?"

"I guess I was in the right place at the wrong time. Some things shouldn't be seen by one this young. I took her away before she could witness the evil of man. Before she could experience the sorrow of loss."

"I know you've taken her to your realm, Klor," said Briathos, striding towards them. "Elspeth. Where did Klor take you yesterday? He took you through a portal. What happened?"

"Klor took me to the moon. It was nice."

Briathos frowned. "What are you up to, Klor?"

"Some things *should* be seen by one this young. Together, we've seen the beauty bestowed upon this land. The mountains, the seas, the forests. The moon was just a little fun. She deserves to see her world before...you know...moving to the next..."

"Then she doesn't know?" asked Briathos.

"Find me her parents, and she doesn't need to know," replied Klor.

"Know what?" asked Elspeth.

"Elspeth, dear girl. You're..."

"ENOUGH!" roared Klor. "Find the parents. I suspect your kind have already taken them to the heavens. Once you have them, return here with them."

"I can't let you take the girl again, Klor."

"You can't stop me." Klor snarled and spread out his wings. "Stand back, Elspeth." Elspeth let go of Klor and ran back a few paces. Eyes wide, she watched as Briathos and Klor circled one another.

"Stop it!" she screamed. Klor and Briathos looked at her, then at one another.

"Sorry, Elspeth," said Klor. He held up his hands. "Let's not be hasty, Briathos. I know you are the 'thwarter of demons', but we have the same goal."

"Then hand over the girl to me."

"I have unfinished business. Bring the parents, and you can take them all together. The way that they *should* move on."

"I'm not in the habit of making deals with demons, but I offer you this, Klor." Briathos raised his hand to the sky. A beam of golden light appeared and enveloped Elspeth. "I've given her divine protection. I suspect I know what business you wish to attend to, and though I don't agree with it, I can understand. Go. Take care of your business, and I'll meet you back here with her parents. I promise she will be safe within the light."

"Are you going to be alright here, Elspeth?" asked Klor.

"Yes. Just please don't fight. It's scary."

"I'm sorry. I never wanted you to be scared."

"It's alright, Klor. I think I understand

everything now. I'm dead, aren't I?"

Klor scowled at Briathos.

"Yes, Elspeth. I'm sorry. I didn't think you needed to know."

"You did what you thought was right. There is just one thing I don't understand. I thought demons were evil. Why are you helping me?"

"I'm curious myself," said Briathos.

"Despite what 'Briathos, thwarter of demons' would have you believe, angels and demons aren't so different. We both help people to find their way to where they are headed. Had an angel been there when you died, Elspeth, then I wouldn't have taken you with me. But these wars of mankind. So much innocence lost. Briathos and his kind have so much work to do. It's no wonder souls become lost or disturbed. I wasn't about to let that happen to you.

"What separates us demons from the angels is how we respond to the atrocities we witness. Briathos is the *forgiving* kind. I am the *vengeful* kind. Wait here, Elspeth. I won't be long." Klor took off into the sky and disappeared over the horizon.

"Elspeth. I'm afraid your parents are also dead," said Briathos. "Know that they are safe and I will return soon with them."

Elspeth nodded, and Briathos pointed to the sky. A portal appeared. Briathos smiled at her and then took off, disappearing into the portal.

Elspeth patiently waited in her beam of light, taking in the forest scenery.

***

"Elspeth! My girl!" Elspeth's mother ran towards her daughter in the golden beam. Elspeth leapt into her arms.

"Mummy!"

"Oh! My angel!"

"Actually, Briathos is the angel," she replied, smiling and hugging her mother tight.

"You're *our* angel, Elspeth," said her father as he joined his wife and daughter. He knelt down and hugged them both.

"I love you, Mummy. I love you, Daddy."

"We love you too, darling. We've been so worried. Briathos told us you were taken by a demon. You must have been so scared."

"Not really," replied Elspeth. "Klor is

a kind demon. He showed me how beautiful the world is. He wanted me to see it before we move on. You'll meet him soon. He had unfinished business to attend to." Elspeth's parents looked questioningly at Briathos.

"It's true. Klor protected Elspeth from the horror of witnessing her death, and your own. For a demon, he is unusual. He acted with Elspeth's best interests in mind, though I suspect his *unfinished business* will reflect his kind in a more familiar light." His attention turned to the forest. "In fact, here he comes now."

Elspeth and her parents turned to see Klor walking out of the trees. Behind him, he was dragging a man in military uniform, his big, clawed hands clamped around the man's neck.

"Klor!" shouted Elspeth. "You're back."

"Did you think I'd let you leave without saying goodbye?" Klor threw the man to the ground. The man scrambled into a sitting position and stared around at everyone, bewildered.

"Who is that man?" asked Elspeth.

"I know who that man is," said her mother. "He was the one who gave the order to his soldiers to kill us. Why have you brought him here?"

"I wanted a companion for my journey home," Klor replied, winking at the man on the floor. He looked up at Briathos. "You kept your side of the deal. I'll keep mine." Briathos nodded and pointed to the sky.

The portal appeared, swirling in golden light. Klor looked at Elspeth and her family. Elspeth smiled at him.

"It's been a pleasure, Elspeth."

"Thank you, Klor," said Elspeth. "Will I see you again?"

"Maybe. When mankind stops killing one another, maybe I'll have a little time to visit. Glad to see you with your family again. Hope you like your new home."

Klor bowed to Elspeth's parents, then turned to the soldier on the ground. "Let's get you home, then." He pointed to the ground, and the earth tore open, revealing a fiery portal. He once again took the man by the neck and threw him screaming into the fire. Then, with a little wave to Elspeth, Klor dived into the portal, which abruptly closed behind him. Just a little smouldering patch on the ground remained.

"Bye, Klor," whispered Elspeth.

First published in *Chapter 6*, Dastaan World magazine, 2018

ABOUT THE PUBLISHER

BLACK HARE PRESS is a small, independent publisher based in Melbourne, Australia.

Founded in 2018, our aim has always been to champion emerging authors from all around the globe and offer opportunities for them to participate in speculative fiction and horror short story anthologies.

Connect

Website: *www.blackharepress.com*

Twitter: *@BlackHarePress*